BAT'S BIG GAME

Retold by

Margaret Read MacDonald

Illustrated by

Eugenia Nobati

www.av2books.com

Your AV² Media Enhanced book gives you a fiction readalong online. Log on to www.av2books.com and enter the unique book code from this page to use your readalong.

AV² Readalong Navigation

Go to **www.av2books.com**, and enter this book's unique code.

BOOK CODE

Z 1 3 0 5 1 4

AV² by Weigl brings you media enhanced books that support active learning.

First Published by

ALBERT WHITMAN & COMPANY
Publishing children's books since 1919

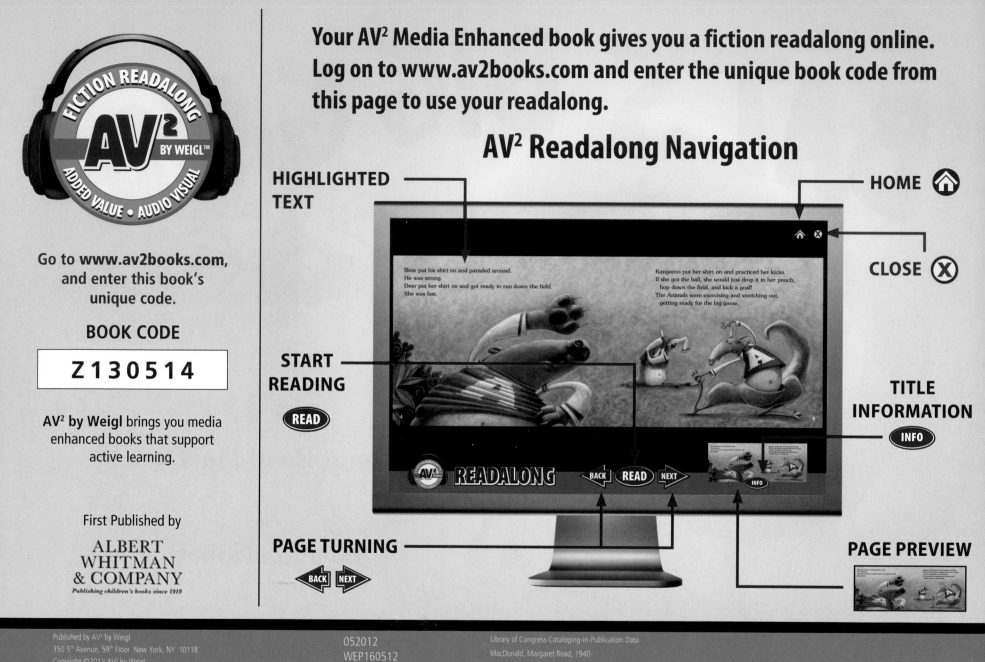

HIGHLIGHTED TEXT

HOME

CLOSE

START READING

READ

TITLE INFORMATION

INFO

PAGE TURNING

BACK NEXT

PAGE PREVIEW

Published by AV² by Weigl
350 5ᵗʰ Avenue, 59ᵗʰ Floor New York, NY 10118

Copyright ©2013 AV² by Weigl

052012
WEP160512

Library of Congress Cataloging-in-Publication Data

MacDonald, Margaret Read, 1940-

Bat's big game / retold by Margaret Read MacDonald ; illustrated by Eugenia Nobati.

p. cm.

Summary: A simplified retelling of the classic Aesop's fable about a ball game between the birds and the animals, and Bat, who wants to play on the winning team.

ISBN 978-1-61913-131-6 (hard cover : alk. paper)

[1. Fables. 2. Folklore.] I. Nobati, Eugenia, ill. II. Aesop. III. Title.

PZ8.2.M16Bat 2012

398.2--dc23

[E]

2012016739

The Animals and the Birds decided to have a ball game.
The Animals came onto the field first.
They had big blue shirts with a great big "A."

Bear put his shirt on and paraded around.
He was strong.
Deer put her shirt on and got ready to run down the field.
She was fast.

Kangaroo put her shirt on and practiced her kicks.
If she got the ball, she would just drop it in her pouch,
   hop down the field, and kick a goal!
The Animals were exercising and stretching out,
   getting ready for the big game.

At the other end of the field, the Birds began to arrive.
Sparrow came. Wren and Robin flew in.
Big Birds, too—Eagle and Ostrich.
Ostrich couldn't fly, but if she got the ball in her beak
  she could *run*.

The Birds all had little red shirts with a little "B."
They put on their shirts and stretched their wings,
  getting ready for the big game!

"We're the BIRDS!
Look at that B!
Birds are gonna win!
B! B! B!"

At the other end of the field, the Animals were ready to go.
"We're the ANIMALS!
Look at that A!
Animals gonna win!
A! A! A!"

In flew Bat. He took a look at those two teams. "Look at those Birds—what a scrawny lot. I don't want to play on the LOSING team.

"Look at those Animals—strong and fast. I'm gonna join the Animal team!"

"Here I am, cousins! Where's my shirt?
I'm ready to play on the Animal team!"
The Animals looked Bat over. "Are you an Animal?"
"What's that folded behind your back? Are those *wings?*"

"Sure, I'm an Animal," said Bat.
"Look at these teeth! Do birds have teeth?
Feel this fur. Do birds have *fur?*
OF COURSE I'm an Animal!"

So the Animals gave Bat a shirt with an "A."

Bat jumped up and down, shouting,

"Go Animals! Gonna win this game! GO! GO! GO! I'm on the winning side!"

13

And the game started!
Bear kicked the ball down the field and made a goal.

14

Then Sparrow took the ball and flew
down the field and made a goal.

15

Then Deer kicked the ball down the field . . .
but Robin snatched it!

16

Robin flew down the field and made another goal!
And the Birds were winning, 2 to 1.

"Uh, oh," said Bat. "Looks like I made a mistake. I'm on the *losing* side! I should have joined the Bird team." Bat took off his Animal shirt and hung it on a bush.

He tiptoed down the field to the Birds' side.
"Hi there, cousins! I've come to join the game!
Where's my shirt? Looks like we're gonna win!"

The Birds looked Bat over. "We didn't know you were a Bird. Weren't you playing for the Animals a minute ago?"

"I'm no Animal," said Bat. "Look at these wings! Do Animals have wings? OF COURSE I'm a Bird!"

So the Birds gave Bat a shirt with a B.

"Go Birds! Gonna win this game!
GO! GO! GO!
I'm on the winning side!"

The game started again.
Wren got the ball
and flew down the field
and made a goal.

Deer got the ball
and ran down the field
and made a goal.

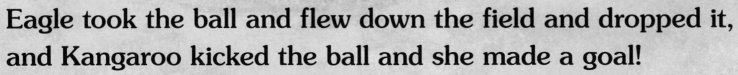

Eagle took the ball and flew down the field and dropped it,
and Kangaroo kicked the ball and she made a goal!

24

Now the Animals had the ball.
Raccoon passed to Kangaroo.
Kangaroo kicked another goal!
And the Animals were leading, 4-3!

CARLETON PLACE
PUBLIC LIBRARY

A B
4 3

"Uh, oh," thought Bat. "These Birds are losing.
I'd better switch back to the Animal team."
Bat took off his Bird shirt and hung it on a bush.
He tiptoed up the field . . . put on his Animal shirt . . .
    and ran back into the game, shouting,

"Go Animals! Gonna win this game! GO!GO!GO! I'm on the winning side.!"

"Wait a minute!" Bear stopped the game.
"Eagle, bring your Birds over here.
Animals, you all come here!"

"Look at this Bat.

Wasn't he playing on the Bird team a minute ago?"

"Yes . . . he was," said the Birds.

"And wasn't he playing on the Animal team a while ago?" asked Bear.

"Yes . . . he was," said the Animals.

"Well, Bat, which side are you on? Are you a Bird or an Animal?"

Everyone waited.

"Well . . . I just wanted to play on the winning side," mumbled Bat.

"I'm sorry for you, Bat," said Bear. "But a good player sticks with the team . . . even when they are *losing*.

Looks like you are not on *any* side now."

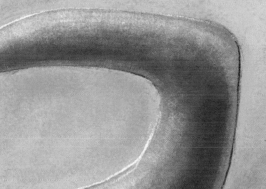

Bat gave back the shirt with the "A."
Bat gave back the shirt with the "B."

And Bat left the field.

"BAT WANTS TO WIN...
GO ... GO ... GO!"

They say Bat is still practicing his game.
I'm not sure which side he plans to play on.
But that's the last time he'll play both sides at once!